Knottypine Mysteries

Mr. Beaverton and the Pistachio Fiasco

By

Olivia Rian

Illustrated by

Sara Aycock

ACKNOWLEDGMENTS

I would like to thank all my wonderful readers who provided helpful feedback: Caroline Stanfield, Lauren, Lillia, and Jack Allred, Ruby and Gordon Aycock, Mike Holweger, Elizabeth Harmon, Jerry Elkins, Joyce Lopez, and Jami Nichols. A thousand thank yous (and a hug) to my husband for his incredible support and his many edits and ideas. Also, for taking care of our kids during the long hours of writing and revising. Finally, a *huge* thank you to Sara Aycock. Knotty Pine Mysteries would have never been created without her artwork and her vision for this project.

— Olivia Rian —

I cannot express enough gratitude to my family, who has always been supportive of my journey to become an artist. A thank you to Colby at Freak Alley Gallery (Boise, ID) who gave me a chance when I needed it most. To Craig and Thomas at Roots Family History (Boise, ID) who have done an amazing job scanning and preparing my artwork. And to God for giving me wings to fly.

— Sara Aycock —

ISBN-13: 978-1548868789

ISBN-10: 1548868787

First paperback edition August 2017

Follow us on social media @knottypinemysteries

For Ken Stanfield, who encourages me to develop my talents and shoot for the stars.

— O.R.

For Sgt. Maj. George M. Earley, who, like Grandfather Beaverton, taught me persistence, hard work, and confidence.

— S.A.

Mr. Beaverton
beaver
(Castor canadensis)

Sheriff Ovis
big-horned sheep
(Ovis canadensis)

Miss Di Delphi
opossum
(Didelphis marsupialis)

Dr. Hoot
great horned owl
(Bubo virginianus)

Oscar Otter
river otter
(Lontra canadensis)

Sir Sly Sepluv
red fox
(Vulpes vulpes)

Corvus
crow
(Corvus brachyrhynchos)

Quilliver Pine
porcupine
(Erethizon dorsatum)

Lady Eden and cubs, Huckle and Berry
black bear
(Ursus americanus)

Miss Sylvi
cotton-tail rabbit
(Sylvilagus nuttallii)

Albert Cornwall
squirrel
(Tamiasciurus hudsonicus)

Topsy and Turvy
box turtle & snail
(Terrapene c. carolina
& Cornu aspersum)

Flavia

yellow-bellied marmot

(Marmota flaviventris)

Mini and Mia

chipmunk

(Tamias minimus)

Hoover Hedgehog

hedgehog

(Erinaceus europaeus)

Toma

woodrat

(Neotoma cinerea)

Ms. Olug
wolverine
(Gulo gulo)

Daguerre
raccoon
(Procyon lotor)

Contents

"Between every two pine trees

there is a door

leading to a new way of life."

— John Muir

1

Night Flight

Mr. Beaverton rested comfortably in his bed of woodchips and held his favorite book between his paws. He looked up at the beams of moonlight shining through his lodge window. The river rippled against the sides of his home and swished soothingly underneath him.

He turned his head to gaze at a painting of his grandfather hanging on the wall in his feeding chamber. His grandfather had always walked with him along the banks of Cobble Creek and explained how the land was healthy because of their dams. Lit by the moonlight, the eyes of the painting stared at Mr. Beaverton through the shadows.

Suddenly, the lodge shook, knocking Mr. Beaver-

ton out of his bed and onto the floor. *"What in the* MOSSY GREEN RIVER CURRENT..." he exclaimed as he scrambled to his feet.

"Mr. Beaverton! MR. BEAVERTON!"

Mr. Beaverton hobbled to the window. He squinted downstream at Sheriff Ovis, a big-horned sheep, who was crammed into a tiny boat. The sheriff threw one end of his rope around a nearby boulder and slowly pulled himself towards the lodge.

Mr. Beaverton poked his head out the window. "Sheriff! *What are you doing out there?"* The lodge rumbled as if in an earthquake.

Dark water sprayed the sheriff as it splashed against the sides of his boat. "I'm leaving Knotty Pine a few days early and heading to Derwood!"

"At this hour?" Mr. Beaverton sputtered, glancing up at the millions of stars in the sky. A wolf began howling in the nearby forest.

"Apparently the town is in a predicament."

Mr. Beaverton scrunched his brow in confusion. "A predicament? What kind?" The sheriff usually spent a couple of weeks in each town of the Evergreen Valley and rarely left a post early, unless another town was having real trouble.

The boat rocked and hit the side of the lodge. "What was that, Mr. Beaverton?"

"WHAT IS *HAPPENING* IN DERWOOD?" Mr. Beaverton shouted as his heart thumped in his chest. He squinted at some sticks from his lodge floating in the water.

"OH! Just break-ins and such. Need to get there quickly, so traveling by river—" Sheriff Ovis took a firmer hold on the rope and secured the side of his boat to the boulder, "—there we go..."

Mr. Beaverton let out a sigh of relief. *"Sticks and bark,* Sheriff! I was beginning to worry you were going to take me and my lodge to Derwood with you."

The extra rope dropped to the ground in a coil at Sheriff Ovis's feet. "As adventurous as that sounds,

Mr. Beaverton, I need you here. As the detective of Knotty Pine, I want you to be *especially* on guard while I make my rounds throughout the valley over the next few weeks."

"I can do that, Sheriff." Mr. Beaverton said as he took a deep breath and rested his paws on the branches lining his window. An evening breeze slowed the pace of his heart. He had kept the town safe many times before. He had even caught a band of squirrels hoarding acorns from Knotty Pine's silo last fall and recovered the town's winter food supply.

"Just be sure to report any suspicious activity while I'm away," Sheriff Ovis added. "I'll stay in Derwood for a couple of weeks and then continue on to Hickory. Just have Morse over at the post office send a telegraph."

"Yes, of course."

"Oh," Sheriff Ovis lowered his voice, "and keep an eye on Sir Sly Sepluv. Shady character."

Mr. Beaverton raised an eyebrow. "The red fox that moved to Knotty Pine a few months ago?"

"Yes, that's the one."

"Why? Not trustworthy?" Mr. Beaverton asked.

Sheriff Ovis sighed. "Hardly. Word is he's been

selling broken, rotten products around town."

Mr. Beaverton nodded, remembering some animals complaining in front of the mercantile a few days ago. "Sure. I'll be watchful of him."

"Thanks, Mr. Beaverton. Oh, and here—" Sheriff Ovis reached for a burlap sack in the boat and tossed it to the window. Mr. Beaverton caught it right before it fell into the river and then reached inside and pulled out a bolt of fine silk. "Your payment for the quarter."

Mr. Beaverton tilted his head. "But this is a lot of silk... do you anticipate more trouble than usual, Sheriff?"

"With break-ins in Derwood, it is possible that Knotty Pine will experience some as well. Just be alert for anything out of the ordinary." Sheriff Ovis reached for the rope that was secured around the boulder.

"Sheriff..." Mr. Beaverton began.

"Good luck, Mr. Beaverton." Sheriff Ovis untied the rope and began floating down the river into the night.

2

The Surprise

M<small>R.</small> Beaverton stretched his arms and looked out his lodge window. The water was back to its mellow swaying, very different from the turmoil caused by the sheriff's boat last night. He wondered if the sheriff had made it to Derwood all right. Maybe he should send him a telegraph.

Mr. Beaverton shuffled to his birch tree table for breakfast. He took a sip of some twig-root tea and rubbed the whiskers on his round chestnut face as he picked up the weekly Knotty Pine newspaper, *The Harvester*.

He began reading through the different headlines. "Knotty Pine's Huckleberry Pie Eating Contest Results." He had lost this year, even though he had

eaten six whole pies! Maybe next year. He read on...
"Budding New Business Hoover's Haberdashy and
Mercantile Branches Out" and then "Lady Eden's
Sore Foot Remedy Heals Throughout Evergreen Val-
ley."

He sipped some more tea and flipped the newspaper to the international section. He skimmed the first
article:

The Harvester
International News

July 16, 1852

VIOLENT CRIMINAL ON THE LOOSE

NEW YORK CITY, NY—
Dangerous predator, Vipera
Berus, escaped from custody
in London nearly three months
ago and continues to evade
capture.

Although investigation by
London police remains under-
way, a dock employee at the
Port of New York recently
discovered a snakeskin match-
ing the description of Berus
in cargo originating from the
United Kingdom.

Police request that all citizens be cautious in the unlikely
event of meeting the fugitive.

Last spring, Berus was
found guilty of trading pistachios mixed with a similar yet poisonous nut known
as the betel. Numerous customers have suffered from
horrid bellyaches, and at least
71 animals with severe cases
have been admitted to the
Royal London Hospital.

Berus was also charged
with vulpicide and arson but
was never convicted.

Please report any poten-
tial leads to your local sheriff.

Mr. Beaverton finished reading. He had never heard of the betel nut, although he had recently tried pistachios for the first time.

He glanced at the light coming through his window and leapt out of his chair. The sun had already risen over the mountains, which meant that he had spent too much time reading his newspaper! He was supposed to be at his office by now, and Sheriff Ovis was counting on him to keep the town safe.

He buttoned his gray waistcoat, grabbed his cane, and dove into his underwater tunnel to the river.

Once on the banks of Cobble Creek, Mr. Beaverton shook the water from his waistcoat. He hurried past the pine trees and grassy knolls leading to town, stopping only once to gnaw on some tasty-looking aspen bark.

As he walked into the center of Knotty Pine, he saw many animals working and enjoying the rising sun. Lady Eden, a black bear, and her cubs were selling nuts, berries, and herbs from a cart. Hoover, a hedgehog, was setting up a display of new fabrics and clothing styles in front of his shop, Hoover's Haberdashy and Mercantile. Daguerre, a raccoon, was taking images of animals, buildings, and trees with his large, box-shaped camera.

Mr. Beaverton glanced up at the sign *Mr. Beaverton's* over the entrance to his office and shuffled inside. He hoped to find his secretary Miss Di Delphi, an opossum, ready with a pot of her delicious red berry tea.

But, her desk was empty.

He sniffed the air and looked closely around the room. Miss Di's bureau near her desk appeared as normal, full of yarn and stacks of parchment as well as hats and oils.

His eyes swept the room. Suddenly, he saw the purple of Miss Di's dress on the ground. He jumped back and widened his small eyes at her body lying on the ground, limp. Her paws were curled, and a bit of drool oozed down the side of her mouth.

Mr. Beaverton scampered outside to find Dr. Hoot.

3

The Quill

"SHE's not dead." Dr. Hoot, a great-horned owl, said as he lowered his spectacles and leaned forward for a closer look.

Mr. Beaverton rested on his cane behind Dr. Hoot. He rubbed his chin while examining Miss Di's furry white face. The opossum lay motionless on the floor in her frilly purple dress. "Are you sure?"

Dr. Hoot turned to Mr. Beaverton and stared at him with his startling yellow eyes. He snapped his beak and nodded. "Just stunned. Get me a wet cloth and let's see if we can wake her."

Mr. Beaverton went through the entrance to the kitchen. He breathed in the fragrance of sweet tea. The wash basin and pump next to the little stove

and table were clean. A vase of alpine forget-me-nots stood in the center next to a small bowl of pistachios and almonds. A basket of linens in the corner was nearly empty, except for a couple of cotton washcloths.

Mr. Beaverton took a washcloth to dip into the basin. As he began to wet the cloth, he noticed porcelain fragments and a handle at the bottom of the water. He brought his spectacles to his nose and gazed into the water. He looked upward at the shelf above the wash basin, where more small pieces of porcelain lay. He ran his paw across the wood, noting it was smooth like a river stone.

"Beaverton!" Dr. Hoot squawked.

Mr. Beaverton lifted his head right into the shelf above him with a loud thud. "Agh! *Paw slivers!*" He rubbed his head and then quickly dipped the wash-cloth into the basin.

As he scurried back to the front room, he stumbled over his feet. *"PAW SLIVERS!"* he exclaimed again.

Dr. Hoot glanced up from laying a cushion under Miss Di's head. "What was that?"

Mr. Beaverton limped as he walked to Dr. Hoot. "Oh, nothing; I just tripped, Doc."

"But I could have sworn I heard—do you have a sliver, Mr. Beaverton? Risk for infection, you know."

"What?"

"You said *'paw slivers!'*" Dr. Hoot explained.

"Oh, that! Just a family expression. Don't you hate it when you are gnawing on a nice piece of bark and..." Mr. Beaverton's voice trailed off as he noticed Dr. Hoot's blank stare. He sheepishly passed the washcloth to Dr. Hoot and retreated to a chair to rub his sore foot. Dr. Hoot dabbed Miss Di's head. She did not stir under the touch of the wet cloth.

Mr. Beaverton stood, slowly putting weight on his foot, and began pacing around the small room. Miss Di's baskets were tidy on the shelves, as usual. He stopped in front of her desk and saw several scattered telegraphs that she had received in the last few weeks, mostly updates from the surrounding towns that she had already shown to him. He noticed a buckram-bound copy of *The Caper of the Hazelnuts, Forensics 101,* and some newspapers in the corner.

"And you found her like this?" Dr. Hoot asked as he continued to dab Miss Di's forehead.

Mr. Beaverton turned from the desk and nodded. "I came in for work, as usual, and found her lying on the ground." Mr. Beaverton paused. "Why do you think she was stunned, Doc?"

Dr. Hoot distractedly rubbed his wing over his head. "It's hard to say. Opossums can appear unconscious when frightened—*thanatosis*—it's a natural reaction." He brushed the washcloth along the sides of Miss Di's face. "But, I think she would have responded to us by now if that were the case."

"Well, I think I found some clues in the kitchen that might explain what happened."

Dr. Hoot rotated his head around 180 degrees to

face Mr. Beaverton. *"Who-oo!* Like what?"

Mr. Beaverton jumped back. "D-Doc!! Don't do that! It's quite... unsettling."

Dr. Hoot tilted his head. "Unsettling, eh? Do you have a fever coming on, Mr. Beaverton? Could be that sliver..." He turned his head back towards Miss Di and lightly put his wing to her head as she began to stir. "Ah, she's waking."

Miss Di blinked at Dr. Hoot and Mr. Beaverton hovering above her. "W-what happened?" She trembled as she tried to sit up, but Dr. Hoot gently guided her back onto the cushion.

"Are you okay, Miss Di?" Mr. Beaverton asked as he leaned in closer.

She wiped her head with her paw. "I—I think so," she stuttered.

"Do you remember anything about this morning?"

Miss Di closed her eyes. "Well, yes. I made some red berry tea—I had a slight stomachache. Then I filed some of your latest reports to send to Sheriff Ovis."

"Do you happen to remember hearing something break?"

Miss Di stared at Mr. Beaverton and slowly nodded. "Yes, a loud crashing noise in the kitchen; it. . . it startled me—"

"—and you went into shock," Dr. Hoot finished.

Mr. Beaverton rubbed his round rose. "Well, it was a pitcher. Several pieces fell into the wash basin when it shattered. I called for Dr. Hoot right after I found you on the ground."

Miss Di stood slowly with the help of Dr. Hoot and her dark eyes skimmed the room. She walked to her desk and moved some paper and ink around. "How peculiar."

"Yes, Miss Di?" Mr. Beaverton stood behind her.

"Of all my possessions," she motioned to her bottles of expensive oil and velvet hats on a bureau by her desk, "my writing quill, with the gold tip, is *gone.*"

"The quill you always have with you for police reports?" Mr. Beaverton asked.

She pulled a handkerchief from her pouch just under the waistband of her skirt and sniffed. "Yes."

"Do you remember where you had it last?"

"I was finishing those reports and writing memos this morning. So, here at my desk," Miss Di said.

"Don't worry, Miss Di. I don't have any other cases today, so I should have plenty of time to get to the bottom of this—" Mr. Beaverton turned his head as he heard a small scratch at the doorway.

Oscar stood in the entrance of Mr. Beaverton's office. " 'Cuse me, Mr. Beaverton?"

"Uh, yes, Oscar?" Oscar was a young otter who was found on the banks of Cobble Creek last spring with no memory of his family or home. Mr. Beaverton had taken him in as a tenant, and Oscar had offered to help him with cases in return.

Oscar scratched his nose. "I was just at school. Berry, Lady Eden's cub, had her brand-new lunch pail stolen."

"How strange! First the quill, and now a pail. . ."

"A quill too?" Oscar asked loudly.

"Yes, one moment, Oscar." Mr. Beaverton turned to Miss Di. "If you'll excuse me, I think I should head to the schoolyard with Oscar. It's possible the animal who stole your quill also stole the pail."

"Oh, I can help investigate, Mr. Beaverton," she said eagerly.

"You go ahead and rest, Miss Di."

She tossed her handkerchief and straightened. "I'm fine, really. I can work."

Mr. Beaverton shook his head. "Please, Miss Di.

Just for the day. You might be injured. Right, Dr. Hoot?"

Dr. Hoot tapped his wing on his beak. "Well, she seems fine now. But, you can never be too careful after a fainting spell like this."

Miss Di sighed in disappointment and sat at her desk, resting her cheek on her paw.

Mr. Beaverton patted her shoulder briefly before grabbing his top hat and pointing his cane. "Off we go, Oscar!"

4

The Agreement

MR. Beaverton squinted at the sun shining brightly over Knotty Pine as he shuffled out of his office with Oscar. He could almost feel the cool morning mist that drifted over the purple peaks of the Bluebird Mountains. His eyes wandered to Cobble Creek and the Howling Forest on the opposite side of town. The trees were dipping their low branches into the refreshing water.

They began walking to the schoolhouse. Lady Eden waved from her herb cart where she was assembling a twill sack of seeds. Oscar grabbed his penny-farthing bicycle as Toma, a woodrat and Knotty Pine's librarian, scurried past them with a stack of books and a few knickknacks poking out of her bag.

Mr. Beaverton turned to Oscar. "So, Berry lost a special lunch pail?" he asked. They passed a few animals who were browsing a display of new dresses and breeches in front of Hoover's Haberdashy and Mercantile. Although the store had only opened a few months ago, it was always bustling with animals.

"I heard her sayin' somethin' about a flower collection inside of it." Oscar pulled a piece of fish out of his pocket and popped it into his mouth as they walked.

Mr. Beaverton's ear twitched as he peered at the hotel, the Pine Lodge. Sir Sly Sepluv, a red fox, and Corvus, a crow, were sitting by the entrance having a conversation. Mr. Beaverton rubbed his chin. He should be more watchful of Sly like the sheriff had ordered, especially with property going missing. He turned to Oscar. "Would you go ahead, Oscar? I'll meet you at the school in a few minutes."

"Alrighty!" Oscar said as he hopped onto his bicycle and rode off.

Mr. Beaverton began walking and tipped his hat to Turvy, an eastern box turtle. Turvy sat lazily in front of his restaurant, Topsy Turvy's, with his burnt-orange shell gleaming under the sun. A chipmunk wearing a smock rushed a bowl of raspberries and carrots to a pot of soup that hung over the fire pit in front of the restaurant. Mr. Beaverton's mouth watered as he watched the carrots and raspberries fall into the pot. He thought about the smell of delicious soup that would soon be filling that corner of the town.

As Mr. Beaverton reached the Pine Lodge, Sir Sly Sepluv slid off a barrel. Corvus flapped his wings and perched on a windowsill near Sly's head. Sly's golden eyes narrowed and his mouth pulled into a smirk as Mr. Beaverton drew near. "Why, Beaverton, already patrolling the streets so early? You're Ovis's little pawn... Aren't you supposed to be with Miss Di?" Sly sneered.

Mr. Beaverton stopped a few feet in front of the barrel. *"Interesting* you mention that, Sly. That's why I've come to talk to you."

Sly flipped his tail. "I've been with Corvus all morning."

Corvus cawed and jumped onto the barrel. "It's true. We've been, um, working."

Mr. Beaverton leaned on his cane. "Right. So, you know nothing about Miss Di's missing quill?"

Sly barred his teeth as he began cackling. "I wouldn't take a quill."

"Even a golden quill?" Mr. Beaverton asked.

Sly snorted as he leaned on the edge of the barrel. "What are you doing, Beaverton? I heard about that 'case' you tried to solve last fall with the acorn depletion."

"This is different." Mr. Beaverton paused as the heat began to rise in his face. "And the bottom fact is I *did* solve that!" He might have had a couple mishaps, sure. But, he had saved the acorns. He glanced at his permanently injured foot.

"Yes, quite the crisis. From what I heard, you found a couple of greedy squirrels filling their sacks with those *precious* acorns," Sly said with a huff.

"Which many animals eat all winter," Mr. Beaverton shot back while folding his arms.

Corvus hopped off the barrel and checked his pocket watch. "Well! I must be going. Traveling today, deliveries to make." He squinted at the clouds gathering in the sky.

"Don't forget this," Sly said as he bent to the ground to pick up a couple pistachios that had fallen out of a small red bag. Sly passed the bag to Corvus.

"Right." Corvus placed the small bag in the pocket of his vest. "Sly, Beaverton." Corvus flew off towards the woods, his watch swinging by the chain in his claw.

Sly straightened the vibrant blue and green peacock feather in his hat. "Well, it's been nice, *detective.*"

Mr. Beaverton paused, considering how he could keep an eye on the tricky fox while continuing the investigation. He couldn't be two places at once... He held up a paw. "Hold on, Sly. I have a proposition for you."

Sly licked his lips. "What could you *possibly* want with me?"

Mr. Beaverton tucked his cane under his arm. "I want you to investigate with me today. Figure out who *is* causing trouble here in Knotty Pine."

"What trouble? A missing quill?" Sly rolled his eyes.

"And lunch pail," Mr. Beaverton added.

"A lunch pail?"

"Sly, this is serious! I want your help."

Sly laid down, his brown plaid jacket resting on the dirt. "And why would I do that?"

Mr. Beaverton remembered his last payment from the sheriff. "Well, I—I have a yard of fine silk. It's yours if you help me find the thief. You could use it to make a new cravat."

"Not interested."

Mr. Beaverton lowered his eyebrows impatiently. "Oh, what else are you going to do today? Trade in the Howling Forest? Dig holes?" He had seen Sly digging just last week to find a breakfast of earthworms.

Sly's whiskers twitched. "I'll think of something."

Mr. Beaverton lifted his shoulders. "Well, alright.

I guess I'll take my offer elsewhere."

Sly yawned loudly. "Yes, I guess so."

Mr. Beaverton paused. Maybe Sly would respond to flattery. "Sly, I could really use your... assistance. Don't you have investigative experience?"

"None whatsoever."

Mr. Beaverton stared at him for a long moment. "How can I convince you?"

Sly blew out a breath. "Maybe if you stop *annoying* me. Why do you need help again?"

Mr. Beaverton glanced over his shoulder at the restaurant, mercantile, and library leading to the schoolhouse before looking back at Sly. "Oscar's in school today. I could use an extra set of eyes. *And* Miss Di is recovering from her fall this morning."

Sly exhaled again. *"Three* yards then."

"Done!" Mr. Beaverton said as he reached his paw out to shake on the agreement. Sly ignored the gesture.

Sly stood and brushed the dirt from his fur while eyeing the gold buttons on his jacket. "And I want to see this silk."

"First—" Mr. Beaverton said, lifting his cane, "to the schoolyard!"

5

The Pail

YOUNG rabbits, mice, raccoons, turtles, squirrels, wolf pups, and bear cubs played around the entrance of the weathered schoolhouse. Mr. Beaverton and Sly passed a group of jackrabbits chasing one another and pushing an old ball around. Some mice and squirrels skittered around picking daisies and bright blue chicory. Oscar and Quilliver, a porcupine, sat on the steps and leafed through a textbook about dangerous predators. Quilliver excitedly reached his paw over to draw Oscar's attention to an interesting paragraph. Oscar inched his head closer to the book but kept his body away from the quills poking out of Quilliver's worn, yellow jacket.

Berry sniffled while she sat on the steps of the

schoolhouse. Her twin, Huckle, bounded to her with a wildflower, hoping to cheer her up.

Sly wrinkled his nose and sat down in some grass away from the squeaking and barking of the playing animals. Shuffling around the schoolyard, Mr. Beaverton sniffed inside mossy logs and mountain laurel shrubs. He gnawed at a curious piece of wood, still damp from the morning dew. Then he pulled out his spectacles and studied a knot in a nearby tree. Sly sauntered up behind him.

"I doubt the lunch pail is in there."

Mr. Beaverton grunted. "I know."

Sly placed his paw on the bark and peered into the dark hole. "Then why waste your time?"

Mr. Beaverton folded his arms. "Any branch, hole, or basket could reveal potential evidence."

Sly shrugged and picked up Mr. Beaverton's cane. "Why do you carry this, anyway? You don't need it." He waved the cane over his head, narrowly missing a tree.

"Careful with that!" Mr. Beaverton snatched it back. "My right foot gets sore. And, it's a family heirloom."

"A *cane?*"

Mr. Beaverton pivoted as he heard a rustling in the grass. Berry stood with her paws behind her back and her eyes focused on the ground. "Mr. Beaverton?"

"Yes, Miss Berry?"

"I—I left my lunch pail just on the side of the schoolhouse, near the hill."

"Thank you, Berry. And when you returned it was gone?"

"Yes. I'll show you." She led them to the other side of the schoolhouse. Sly sniggered as Mr. Beaverton tripped over a stray branch.

As they passed the entrance, Oscar glanced up from his book and his mouth dropped open. He scurried over to Mr. Beaverton and whispered, *"Why is Sly with you?"*

"I have a couple reasons, Oscar. I'll explain later," Mr. Beaverton replied.

Oscar scratched his head. "Well, his 'world famous raspberries' he sold me last week were pretty rott'n..." He paused. "But not too rott'n to eat!" He reached inside his pockets for a snack.

As they neared the side of the schoolhouse, Berry pointed to a patch of smashed grass next to a couple

of pails that were covered in rust and smudges of dirt. "I left my new pail there and went to go climb a tree with Squirrella and Huckle. I came back to put a pawful of white clover that we picked into my pail and it was gone."

Mr. Beaverton bent down to the grass for a closer look. A small tuft of gray fur sat on top of a flattened area. He picked up a few strands and brought them to his nose, noting a strange but familiar odor. He re-examined the ground. A few pistachios were scattered like pebbles in the grass.

"Beaverton," Sly said as he pointed to some small tracks in the dirt.

Mr. Beaverton looked curiously at the tracks and then up as he felt movement on the ground.

Miss Sylvi, a mountain cottontail rabbit, hopped to where they stood. "Hello, Mr. Beaverton. Are you here about the pail?"

Mr. Beaverton tipped his hat. "Good morning, Miss Sylvi. And yes, Oscar just informed me. Has it been missing long?"

Miss Sylvi straightened her brown ears. "Just in the last hour. She has been quite upset. Thank you for coming."

"Of course. Has anything else gone missing today?"

"Not that I've noticed."

Mr. Beaverton rubbed his chin. "Hmm... and nothing peculiar around the school today while you've been teaching? Nothing out of the ordinary?"

"No, not that I can recall; normal school day. Some students are taking a recess while others are in the woods finishing their plant identification assignment," Miss Sylvi replied.

"Do your students have assignments in the woods often?"

"Yes," Miss Sylvi said. "There's so much to learn and discover among the plants and trees—"

Just then, a young mouse and one of the jackrabbits bounded to Miss Sylvi. "Teacher!"

Miss Sylvi turned. "Yes?"

"We found strange tracks in the woods," they said together.

"Really? What kind?" Miss Sylvi asked.

"We're not sure," the mouse squeaked, "but long lines in the dirt."

"We want you to come see." The jackrabbit bounced excitedly.

"Patience, patience." Miss Sylvi turned to Mr. Beaverton. "Do you have any other questions for me?"

"No, no questions. But you and your students stay safe until we can crack this case."

She nodded and hopped behind her students into the woods.

Mr. Beaverton turned to Oscar. "You can stay at school, Oscar. I'll find you later if I need you."

Oscar pursed his lips in Sly's direction for a moment. "Sure, alrighty," he said and leapt over to Quilliver. They left to finish their assignment.

"So, Sly, what kind of tracks do you think you found earlier?"

Sly raised his shoulders. "From a rodent, perhaps?"

"A rodent? Hmm—" Mr. Beaverton pivoted as he heard the thumping of footsteps and the cracking of twigs behind him. "Ah, there you are, Mr. Beaverton." Miss Di marched swiftly towards them while pulling a commonplace book out of her pouch. Dust flew around her in a flurry as she took each step.

"Miss Di!" Mr. Beaverton exclaimed. "Shouldn't you be resting?"

"Please, Mr. Beaverton; I'm okay, really." She brushed off the dust that had gathered on her skirt and opened her book. "What did I miss?"

"We just investigated the schoolyard and searched for the missing pail," Mr. Beaverton replied.

Miss Di took note in her book and side-glanced at Sly. "What's *he* doing here?"

Mr. Beaverton watched Sly yawn. "Just helping me since Oscar is in school."

"Oh. But, he doesn't even work for you," she said while a breeze teased at the feather on her hat.

"I know."

Miss Di scrunched her nose. "So, anything interesting?"

Mr. Beaverton leaned on his cane. "No sign of the

pail. But we did find some gray fur and small tracks where the pail had been taken."

"Well, that narrows down the suspects... You never know though, the thief may be trying to lead us off their trail." Miss Di wrote in her book. She then looked up and cleared her throat. "Well, I'll just look around... for the police report."

Mr. Beaverton rubbed his chin. "Okay, if you're really sure you're feeling well enough. We'll be heading back to the center of town." He paused. "Be careful." He didn't want her passing out again if she wasn't feeling well.

"I will." Miss Di licked her paw and brushed at her fur before walking around the schoolyard.

Sly scratched his nose. "Where do we go next, Beaverton?"

"I'm not sure. Let's just hope we find more clues so we can figure out what's going on around here before something else goes missing." Mr. Beaverton began trudging down the dirt path and motioned for Sly to follow.

6

The Silver

As Mr. Beaverton and Sly passed the library into the center of town, Albert, a squirrel, and publisher of *The Harvester* newspaper, bounded to them.

"Good morning, Albert," Mr. Beaverton said as he tipped his hat. "Interesting international article in the newspaper this week."

"Mr. Beaverton! Oh, yes, I've been following that pistachio case for a few months now..."

"That evidence they found in New York is concerning." Mr. Beaverton tapped his chin. "Any sign of the betel nut getting mixed with pistachios here in America?"

"Hmm... as far as I know, no one has gotten sick." Albert gulped as he glanced back at his print shop.

"Anyway, Mr. Beaverton—I've actually been trying to reach you for half an hour!"

Mr. Beaverton raised his eyebrows. "Why, what happened?"

"I heard about the thieveries today and went out to interview the victims for a story." Albert's squeaky voice rose as he spoke. "When I came back to my press to start drafting the story, I noticed a pawful of my metal printing letters missing!"

Mr. Beaverton blew out a breath. "Seriously? *Another* theft, already?"

Albert glanced to Sly and twitched his tail. "Has he been with you all day?"

Sly muttered through his teeth. *"Definitely for the past hour..."*

Mr. Beaverton stepped quickly in front of Sly. "We can come examine your shop, Albert. Have you seen Daguerre this morning?"

Albert straightened his blue bow tie and vest as his eyes flitted from Sly back to Mr. Beaverton. "Yes. He's been around taking images for me to refer to for my next article."

"Please tell him to come find me next time you see him."

"Sure," Albert said as they began walking to the print shop.

"Wow," Sly snickered.

Mr. Beaverton raised his shoulders. "What?"

"This town gets a pen, a pail, and a couple of letters stolen and it's all *mayhem*."

Albert puffed his chest as he removed his bowler hat and shook it at Sly. "Those printing letters are important for my newspaper! Try spelling 'Knotty Pine' or *'The Harvester'* without a 'V' or a 'Y'!"

Mr. Beaverton looked at Sly. "You see, Sly, in a small town, stolen valuables are quite the mishap."

"How tragic," Sly said as a breeze lifted his hat from his head.

Mr. Beaverton stopped in front of the mercantile and cocked his head towards Sly. "And I assume you lived in a bigger town before you moved here?"

Sly laughed. "Town? More like a metropolis compared to this little place." He repositioned his hat.

"But you didn't like it there?"

Sly narrowed his eyes suspiciously. "Why do you ask?"

Mr. Beaverton pursed his lips. "Just curious."

Sly blew out a breath. "Well, it's a long story.

And we clearly have more important work to attend to here. We can't have more letters getting stolen from the local print shop." He rolled his eyes as Albert folded his arms and scowled.

They continued to walk past Hoover's Haberdashy and Mercantile and around the fire pit in front of Topsy Turvy's Restaurant. A slow, booming voice interrupted them.

"Miiiister Beeaaavertooon, maaay I haaave aaa woooord?"

Mr. Beaverton stopped next to Turvy, who was stirring a pot of soup over his fire pit. Being an old turtle, Turvy spoke as quickly as he walked. "Certainly, Turvy. What can I do for you?" Mr. Beaverton licked his lips at the aroma of the carrot and raspberry soup that lingered in the air.

"Miiiissing siiilver iiin the kiiiitchen. Juuust poooliiished yeeesteerdaay. Pleeeaaase cooome loooook."

"Sour water! This will be the *fourth* theft today!" Mr. Beaverton exclaimed.

"Foooouur? Hooooow uuunfooortunaate. Dooo yoouuu haaave aaa moooment tooo cooome iinsiide?"

"Please do, Beaverton, so he'll stop talking," Sly

muttered.

"Hmm... Do you mind, Albert, if we go investigate?" Mr. Beaverton asked.

Albert bounced on his feet. "Go ahead, but hurry. I'll see you soon..." He bounded off to the print shop.

The double doors creaked as Mr. Beaverton and Sly entered Topsy Turvy's Restaurant. Mr. Beaverton breathed in fruit and spice and squinted at a fire crackling in the corner. They passed several mice playing a cheerful tune on a piano.

Mr. Beaverton tossed his hat onto Topsy the snail's back. "Nice shot mister—" Topsy began.

"Riiiight theeere iiin theee baaack, thaaanks," Turvy said behind them.

"—Hey, I was talking you overgrown turtle!" Topsy shouted.

"Yooouuu juuusst keeeep caaatchiiing thooose haaats, yooou muustaachioed eescaargoot..."

"Why, I outta make turtle soup be tomorrow's special!" Topsy grinned as he adjusted his faux mustache.

Mr. Beaverton chuckled at the two as he shuffled

into the kitchen. He could smell a hint of cinnamon in the air. Sly followed behind him.

A couple of chipmunks and a yellow-bellied marmot wearing white smocks peeked up from chopping vegetables on a long table in the center of the small room. Several other chipmunks scurried back and forth from the dining room.

Mr. Beaverton approached the yellow-bellied marmot. "Excuse me, miss..."

"Miss Flavia. I'm the chef."

"Miss Flavia, where were you all when the silver was taken?"

The marmot lifted her shoulders. "Well, we all come in and out so often and so quickly, we didn't notice anything out of the ordinary. Mini just went to grab some forks for a table and noticed half of our silverware was gone." She motioned to a chipmunk rushing bowls of soup to the dining room.

"Where do you keep your silverware?"

She pointed to a half-full basket near the wood stove. Mr. Beaverton hunched down and studied the contents. The silver forks and spoons were piled on each other in a haphazard manner, but they were clean. *Except...* he leaned his head closer to the

basket. Tufts of gray fur rested along the sides, and a few scratch marks were present along the rim. He lifted some fur and a pistachio fell to the ground. *Strange.* He sniffed the distinct smell of the fur and put a couple strands into his pocket.

"Aaaany luuuck, Miiiister Beeaaaverton?" Turvy waddled in from the dining room.

"I don't know yet, but I'm on to something."

"Suuure, iiinfoorm meee wheeen yooouu knooow mooore. Woooouuuld yoouu liiike aaa Tooopsy Tu-uurvy Speeeciiaal? Yoouuur graaandfaaatheeer's faaavooriiite, yoouuu knooow."

"Yes, yes, I know. And that would be splendid, Turvy, thank you!"

"Flaaaviaaa, pleeease maaake speeeciiaals fooor

theeesse geeentleeemeen."

"Thank you, Turvy," Mr. Beaverton said again and sat down at the end of the long table.

Sly sat across from Mr. Beaverton. "So, did you find anything, Beaverton?"

Mr. Beaverton took the strands of fur from his pocket. "I found this in the basket of silverware. I found similar fur where the pail had been taken."

Sly brought the strands an inch from his face and scrunched his brow. "What kind of animal has this fur?"

Mr. Beaverton tapped his claw on the table. "It looks familiar, but I can't quite place it. But what's interesting is, no trace of the fur at Miss Di's."

"Maybe the thief was more careful?" Sly asked.

Mr. Beaverton shook his head. "A pitcher was broken there, though."

"Anything else?"

Mr. Beaverton continued to tap the table. "Among the fur and scratch marks, I'm finding traces of pistachios as well."

Sly didn't respond as a couple jittery chipmunks heaved two plates towards them. Each plate held three slices of huckleberry pie stacked on top of each

other with red raspberries and sprigs of mint. "Your specials, sirs!"

Sly popped half a slice of pie into his mouth. His eyes widened as he tasted the sweet yet tart berry filling. "This is *delicious.*"

"So flavorful!" Mr. Beaverton licked the berry juice that dripped off his spoon.

Suddenly, the kitchen doors swung open with force. "There you are!" Miss Di stood at the entrance with her commonplace book in her arms. "What did I miss?"

Mr. Beaverton raised his eyebrows. "Miss Di! How did you know where we were?" She had not been around when Turvy requested to have the missing silver investigated.

"Not important—what are you two doing?" she said as she brushed at her dress.

He motioned to the basket. "Half the silverware was missing. And we found this." He took the fur from his pocket.

Miss Di scribbled furiously in her commonplace book. She then took a turn around the room and peered in the corners and baskets. She walked back to stand in front of Mr. Beaverton and Sly and eyed their pie. "We certainly need to get to the bottom of this. Are you about finished with your pie, Mr. Beaverton?"

Mr. Beaverton took a bite and dabbed his mouth. "Yes, just about. Ready, Sly? We don't want to keep Albert waiting."

Sly swallowed the last of his pie and stood up. "Oh yes, it would be a shame to delay the *all-important* writer of the local newspaper."

Mr. Beaverton grabbed his cane. "He publishes interesting articles. Sometimes even international news, like the recent article about that pistachio criminal." He picked up his hat from Topsy's back on his way out the door. "Good day, Topsy."

"Oh yes, fascinating case," Miss Di commented.

Sly lowered his ears. "I suppose. Let's go."

7

The Buttons

GRAY clouds began to float in front of the sun as the three animals wandered out of Topsy Turvy's Restaurant. Mr. Beaverton closed his eyes and felt the wind rush through his fur. He breathed in the smell of pine that blew down from the mountains. "Beautiful day."

Sly scrunched his nose at the sky. "I suppose. Looks like rain."

Mr. Beaverton tilted his head up to the clouds and shrugged. "Yes, maybe."

Lady Eden left her cart of herbs as she saw Mr. Beaverton shuffle away from the restaurant.

"Mr. Beaverton, thank you for searching for Berry's missing pail," she said as she twirled a black and white umbrella in her paws.

"It's no problem, Lady Eden. We are still investigating the matter." He looked at her cart, full of fruit, roots, nuts, and plants. "Any new herbs today?"

She nodded eagerly. "Yes, I found some wild mint and juniper leaves on the edges of the Howling Forest this morning."

"Mmm, I like to take a little mint when I need to concentrate. I might come by your cart later."

"Well, hold on." She walked quickly to her cart and then back with a small vial of mint extract. "For helping Berry."

"Aspen bark on a sunny day! Thank you, Lady Eden!" He sniffed the fresh mint and placed it into his pocket while Sly rolled his eyes.

"Anytime." Lady Eden brushed her blue dress and walked back to her cart as a chipmunk dashed up and pointed at fresh huckleberries in the fruit section.

Miss Di watched Lady Eden leave and cleared her throat. "Mr. Beaverton... I think I'll head back to the office—to file some of these notes into reports for the day."

Mr. Beaverton lifted his shoulders. "Well, all right. See you later then." Miss Di hurried away to the office. She was acting rather odd today. Maybe she hit her head earlier at the office.

Mr. Beaverton pivoted as he heard footsteps behind him. Hoover, a hedgehog, approached them from his mercantile. "Mr. Beaverton?" He trembled slightly in his red and yellow striped pantaloons.

"Sorry to bother you. I know you've been busy investigating and trying to recover the stolen possessions. I just..."

Mr. Beaverton frowned at Hoover's face, which was looking haggard. "Are you alright, Hoover?"

Hoover took a deep breath. "Yes—it's just, my mercantile... I think the back entrance was broken into."

Mr. Beaverton drew his mouth to the side. "Unfortunately, we've had multiple reports of stolen property today. Anything taken?" Mr. Beaverton briefly wondered if he should send a telegraph to Sheriff Ovis.

Hoover brushed at the spines around his face nervously. "Well, not that I could tell, just a little spilled flour. But, I'd feel a lot better if you'd come check for anything suspicious."

Mr. Beaverton blew out a breath. "We're supposed to meet Albert... but, we can check quickly."

"Thank you," Hoover said as they walked next door to the mercantile.

Mr. Beaverton's waist caught in the door for a moment as they entered the store behind Hoover. *"Rotten wood!"* He picked up the shards of a button that had fallen off his waistcoat.

"What's wrong with you, Beaverton?" Sly sputtered while shaking his head.

"Third button this week," he mumbled before picking at the threads on his waistcoat where the button had been.

Hoover turned and inspected the doorframe. "I don't see anything wrong with the doorway... did you just say, 'rotten wood'?"

"Ah, just an expression—nothing worse than—" Mr. Beaverton watched Hoover scrunch his brow. "Anyway, please, show us what's troubling you," Mr. Beaverton finished quickly.

"Over here, Mr. Beaverton." Hoover pointed to the shelves. "I'm pretty sure the intruder never left the back room, but it wouldn't hurt to check here first."

The mercantile was filled with shelves of fabric, thread, buttons, porcelain, baskets, quilts, and small

toys—some merchandise imported and some hand-crafted by Hoover. A section of parchment and fine ink and quills sat behind jars of honey, berry candy, and peppermint sticks on the desk. In an adjoining room, barrels of seeds, grain, and corn lined the walls.

Mr. Beaverton brought out his spectacles to inspect the shelves behind the counter. After examining each section in the front of the store, he checked the back. He noted long lines in some spilled flour.

"Find anything, Mr. Beaverton?" Hoover asked as he stood in the doorway to the back.

Mr. Beaverton let a pawful of corn fall back into a barrel. "Well, we're not finding the fur or pistachios that we found at the scene of the pail and silverware.

But, there wasn't any at Miss Di's either. I might guess that whoever broke into your place might have broken into Miss Di's as well."

"So, two different criminals?" Sly asked while plopping down in a corner and resting his head.

Mr. Beaverton nodded. "Yes, my guess is we're dealing with two. I also found scratch marks on the silverware basket but no markings here or at Miss Di's. It would have been hard to tell in the grass where the lunch pail was. We'll have to pay attention at Albert's to see if we can draw any more conclusions."

Hoover tapped his paw on his counter. "Well, thank you for checking, Mr. Beaverton. I'll be watchful I suppose."

"Sure, Hoover."

Hoover pointed his paw at the shelves behind him. "Anything I can help you with while you're here? It would be my pleasure."

Mr. Beaverton jiggled the flaps of his waistcoat. "Well, I could use some new buttons."

Hoover went behind the counter and brought out a pine needle basket of colorful buttons. Mr. Beaverton held up several gold, brown, and green buttons in his paw and finally selected a beautiful set of shiny green mussel shell buttons.

Hoover put the buttons in a small burlap sack. "Is that all, Mr. Beaverton?"

"Actually—just wondering, Hoover. Do you often get shipments of pistachios?"

Sly lifted his head up from resting on his arms.

Hoover coughed a couple times and cleared his throat. "Um, not usually. I find they come in more often with traveling salesanimals. Why do you ask?"

"I've just heard recently of betel nuts getting mixed with pistachios. Animals have gotten sick from unknowingly consuming the betel. I'd want you to be careful," Mr. Beaverton replied.

"Of course. Well, luckily, I know the difference. The betel nut is green like a pistachio but noticeably larger..." Hoover's voice trailed off as the bell to the front door rang.

Toma crawled through the entrance with her bag full of books. The apron that rested atop her red cotton dress was soiled from being drug through the dirt. Her small black eyes bulged at the sight of Mr. Beaverton and Sly.

Hoover cleared his throat. "Good afternoon,

Toma. How's the library today?"

Toma bobbed her head once as she focused on the green mussel shell buttons. She then scurried out the door.

Sly cocked his head. "What's with her?"

Mr. Beaverton grunted as he turned from the counter. "That's her normal behavior."

"Unusual."

He shrugged. "She's a woodrat. They're unsocial, solitary, territorial."

"Hmph." Sly sauntered to the door.

Mr. Beaverton sniffed the air at the distinct yet unidentifiable scent. "Well, I think we'll be going. Good luck, Hoover, and let us know if you have any further concerns."

Hoover rubbed the back of his neck. "Thank you."

Mr. Beaverton and Sly walked out of the mercantile. "Now, to Albert's without further delay."

8

The Pine Lodge

MR. Beaverton counted with his claws as they walked along the grassy paths that ran through the middle of town. "So, Miss Di's quill, Berry's pail, Topsy and Turvy's silverware, Albert's letters, and what appears to have been a break-in at Hoover's..."

"Feeling left out, Beaverton? I could swipe your cane if it'd make you feel better," Sly snickered.

Mr. Beaverton ignored him. "We need to find this thief, and soon."

Mr. Beaverton's ear twitched as they passed the Pine Lodge. "I know Albert is waiting, but let's inspect the Pine Lodge while we're close."

Sly snorted. "This town is small, everything is close—" He jumped as a bicycle whizzed past him like a gust of wind on a stormy day.

"Hey, Mr. Beaverton!" Oscar shouted as he hopped off his bicycle.

"Oscar!" he exclaimed. "School out already?"

"Not exactly. After you left, a few students found a snakeskin in the woods. I was just studyin' a book 'bout dangerous predat'rs with Quilliver today..."

Sly yipped. "A snake?"

Mr. Beaverton faced the hotel. "Sounds interesting, Oscar. I'd love to hear more about it, but we really need to investigate the Pine Lodge and get to Albert's."

"But Mr. Beaverton, from studyin' the tail, it has a single row of scales. That means it's ven'omous."

Mr. Beaverton bit his lip. "Well, that is interesting. We do usually only have colubrids come through Knotty Pine."

"Well, the skin is back at the school if you wanna come..."

Mr. Beaverton hesitated and then shook his head. "Sorry, Oscar. Maybe after we investigate the Pine Lodge and print shop. We want to catch this thief before he or she steals again."

Sly coughed. "Err, Beaverton. Maybe we should

check."

Mr. Beaverton raised his eyebrows at Sly. "Well, I appreciate your input," he glanced at Oscar, "Yours as well Oscar. I just *really* think we should continue to the hotel and print shop so we can stop this thief before he or she swipes everything in town."

"Alrighty," Oscar said dejectedly as he climbed onto his bicycle and rode away.

Mr. Beaverton motioned to the Pine Lodge. "Come, Sly."

The Pine Lodge stood high above the other buildings in town. The logs were stacked neatly. A tree extended out of the roof and held special suites with views of the town.

As they entered the front doors, Ms. Olug, a wolverine, stomped up the stairs from her den with her eyes focused on them in a scowl. The scent of pine was strong, but Mr. Beaverton could still smell the musky scent that she brought into the room.

Mr. Beaverton tipped his hat. "Ms. Olug."

"Mr. Beaverton," she responded gruffly.

She turned her head slightly and glared at Sly.

"May I help you?"

Mr. Beaverton stepped forward as Sly took a step back. "Some property has gone missing around town. I was hoping to inspect your rooms, as the thief could be a guest here."

Ms. Olug put a paw on her hip. "Do you have a warrant?"

"Sheriff Ovis has charged me to keep this town safe in his absence. I hope you'll comply."

She hesitated. "Fine. There are four rooms on the main floor, a loft, and then two on top. All of them are occupied except the treehouses."

"Thank you," Mr. Beaverton said.

Ms. Olug grumbled under her breath and clomped back to her den. *"Nocturnal animals always getting disturbed . . ."*

"Wait," Sly turned to Mr. Beaverton as Ms. Olug disappeared down the stairs, "aren't beavers nocturnal as well, Beaverton?"

Mr. Beaverton cleared his throat. "Usually, but I take that mint to keep me alert when I'm working on a case."

"Oh." Sly's tail swished as they began down the hall. "So, we inspecting all these rooms?"

"That's right."

Sly stopped. "And for what again?"

"The missing property... and anything suspicious." Mr. Beaverton stood in front of the first door and knocked lightly.

"Whatever you say, Beaverton."

The first room had cornflowers sprouting up between the floorboards. A family of mice was asleep cozily in a bed of straw in the corner.

Mr. Beaverton's eyes grazed the corners of the room before he whispered, *"Let's move on."*

The second room had a large tree stump right in the middle of the floor. A sleepy bobcat yawned and then began to snore. They quickly searched the room and left.

They tiptoed to the third room where several bluebirds were busy eating a pile of worms. Mr. Beaverton cleared his throat, but they did not peek up from their dinner.

Mr. Beaverton rubbed his chin. "Well, next room, I suppose."

The fourth room was covered in vines. A small waterfall poured out from the far wall, and a frog sat lazily on a lily pad in a pond.

"Excuse us," Mr. Beaverton said.

Ribbit. "Yes?" the frog croaked.

"I'm Mr. Beaverton, detective for Knotty Pine. Have you had an uneventful stay so far?"

Ribbit. "Well, actually, I was having a nightmare about a snake chasing me and trying to eat me. I awoke feeling terrified and thought I saw something slithering across the floor. I couldn't tell if it was real or my imagination though."

Mr. Beaverton rested on his cane. "Anything missing from your room?"

"Not that I could tell." *Ribbit.*

"Be sure to report if so."

Ribbit. "Of course."

As they climbed the stairs, they peeked into the

loft, which was filled with geese. "Can I help you, eh?" A goose close to the entrance honked.

"Err, no." Sly jumped back. "Geese," he muttered.

They climbed the rest of the steps to the top rooms. They searched the smaller treehouse before entering the larger, round room.

Sly walked to a window. "I can nearly see the whole town from here."

They gazed from Topsy Turvy's to Hoover's Mercantile, to the library, and all the way to the schoolhouse while a gust of wind pushed at their fur. They could even see the post office, town hall, jail, and blacksmith shop on the other side of Mr. Beaverton's office.

Mr. Beaverton drummed his paw on the windowsill. "Toma seems to be everywhere but the library today... I wonder why."

Sly turned his head to look at Mr. Beaverton. "Why do you care, anyway?"

"What?" Mr. Beaverton asked, confused.

Sly threw his paws in the air. "About a quill, forks, letters, a *lunch pail...*"

"You've never had a valuable stolen?" Mr.

Beaverton asked.

"If you call those *valuables...*" Sly replied, sarcastically.

Mr. Beaverton sighed and peered out the window before answering. "Do you see my lodge down there, in the middle of Cobble Creek?" Waves splashed against the lodge, but his home stood firm.

"Yes."

Mr. Beaverton stared at his home. "I've lived here my whole life. Built my own lodge a few years ago." He gripped his cane for support. "My grandfather even lived down the stream a little." He took a breath. "Anyway, animals have come and gone. Some have lived here a while, like Dr. Hoot. Others are newer, like you, and Hoover."

Sly lifted his shoulders. "So?"

"I love our small town, nestled at the bottom of the mountains, surrounded by the trees and my creek."

"Oh, Beaverton, you're getting poetic on me."

"And," Mr. Beaverton continued, ignoring him, "I guess I appreciate and respect the animals who live here. They're my friends." He gazed out the window again. "They may not seem like much to you, but they're good, hardworking, resourceful, kind-hearted. . ."

"*I get it*, Beaverton."

"Well," Mr. Beaverton continued, "we take care of each other and keep this community a pleasant place to live. I don't like seeing them unhappy. . . or afraid." He gave a small smile, showing more of his large orange teeth. "My grandfather used to say our town is like a lodge—each town member is a stick or branch that keeps us all together."

"Right. . . Your grandfather—I've heard him mentioned today. What's the deal with him, anyway?" Sly asked.

"I guess he was gone before you moved here. He was a well-loved friend to the animals around Knotty Pine and the surrounding valley. He was a guardian, really—of both the town and land."

Sly eyed his claws. "What happened?"

"He just disappeared this last fall." Mr. Beaverton gulped. "I don't know if he's dead or alive."

Sly brushed at his jacket as wind blew dust through the window. "Any idea why he left?"

Mr. Beaverton lifted his shoulders. "I wish I knew. But, I have a feeling it had something to do with me."

Sly grunted. "Probably."

Mr. Beaverton took a heavy breath and rested his elbows on the window. "Do you like it here, Sly?"

Sly's mouth fell open a little. "It's... fine."

"So, how exactly does your 'business' work? You trade products, with Corvus?"

Sly sniffed. "Usually."

"I've noticed you sell pistachios," Mr. Beaverton remarked.

Sly's eyes narrowed. "Yes."

"Where do you get them?" Mr. Beaverton asked, pointedly.

Sly went rigid and positioned his body away from Mr. Beaverton. "Whoever provides the best deal."

"Well—" Mr. Beaverton suddenly sniffed the air and slapped his tail. He crawled towards the hole leading to the stairs. He stopped for a moment on the rug and sniffed again. "Someone has been here. *Recently.*"

Sly frowned. "Who?"

"I'm not sure. But, from the smell, not Ms. Olug," Mr. Beaverton said as gray clouds floated in from the Howling Forest and cast shadows into the room.

"Strange."

Mr. Beaverton motioned to the stairway. "Let's go—Albert is expecting us."

9

The Images

THE bell on the front door rang as they entered Albert's shop. Mr. Beaverton passed by the printing press. He looked up at the racks of cotton-wood tree paper, made just northeast in Cottonwood Glen. The smell of fresh paper and ink was heavy in the air.

Albert stood up from a chair where he was setting type into the printing press. "Mr. Beaverton—I'm glad you're *finally* here. Daguerre found something interesting in the images that he took today that he wants to show you."

"Excellent. I'll just quickly investigate here and then talk to Daguerre," Mr. Beaverton said as he shuffled to the table where the letters were kept. The

letters were sorted into compartments. He came to the end of the alphabet where some of the letters were missing. He quickly noted more gray fur, scratch marks, and pistachios on the table.

Before walking away, he noticed a couple of newspapers laid out on the table: one copy with a headline about the break-ins in Derwood that Sheriff Ovis had left to investigate and *The Harvester* folded open to the headline about the pistachio criminal.

Mr. Beaverton looked up from the newspapers and cleared his throat. "I think we are definitely onto the thief, Albert. We will do our best to recover your letters."

"Thanks, Mr. Beaverton," Albert said.

"Where is Daguerre?"

Albert pointed to an opening that led to a den below the shop. "Downstairs."

They wandered into a candlelit room. Daguerre, a raccoon, glanced up from a table covered with several silvered copper plates and bottles of iodine. "Over here, Beaverton." He blinked at Sly, but said nothing.

Mr. Beaverton took off his overcoat. He picked up a magnifying glass and a candle from the table and studied the copper plates. There was an image of the schoolyard, an image of Topsy Turvy's Restaurant, and an image of the center of town with the mercantile in the background.

Daguerre motioned to the images. "I've taken several images today, but I found an interesting pattern with these three." Daguerre pointed to the first image. "This was taken this morning, right before I saw you heading to the schoolyard. I was out taking images for a different project, before Albert asked me to focus on the thieveries."

"What is peculiar about this image?" Mr. Beaverton asked. "I notice the trees near the schoolyard..."

Daguerre bounced on his toes and pointed with his paw. "Yes, but near the back of this tree..."

Mr. Beaverton and Sly leaned closer with the magnifying glass.

"You see the tip of a bushy tail," Daguerre continued.

Mr. Beaverton studied the next image as Daguerre pointed and said, "Again, this same tail poking out from behind Topsy Turvy's. Taken when you were on your way there this morning."

"That tail seems familiar." Sly rubbed his chin. "It's not Miss Di or Lady Eden; they're in the other corner of the image."

"Well, it resembles the fur that I've found at the scene of the stolen pail, silver, and letters," Mr. Beaverton remarked.

"That's just it." Daguerre pointed to the last image.

There in the middle of town square was the owner of the tail. Sly turned to Mr. Beaverton in surprise. "The... librarian?"

Mr. Beaverton looked at Sly with wide eyes and nodded. "Toma."

10

The Forest

"WE must speak with Toma at once!" Mr. Beaverton said as he reached for his overcoat and absently put his paws in his pocket. He frowned at his empty paw and poked his head under the table.

Daguerre began to stack the images. "Lose something, Mr. Beaverton?"

Mr. Beaverton ran his paw through his pockets again. "As a matter of fact…" His eyes skimmed the ground once again. "My new green buttons are missing." He side-glanced at Sly.

Sly folded his arms and leaned against the wall. "You think I took them?"

Mr. Beaverton pursed his lips. "Well, I didn't. But you are acting awfully defensive."

Sly forced a laugh. "Because I like to steal buttons in my free time."

"Well, you are known to swindle and pickpocket," Mr. Beaverton said.

Sly's eyes darkened. "I trade; there's a difference."

Mr. Beaverton huffed. "Yes, I've heard, Sly. Musty scarves and moldy walnuts."

Sly scowled. "So, is this why you've enlisted me today? To keep an eye on me?"

"Not the only reason... the sheriff..." Mr. Beaverton began.

"Unbelievable!" Sly spun around and stalked out of the room. "My time would be better spent 'trading in the Howling Forest' or 'digging holes,'" he muttered, stomping up the stairs.

Mr. Beaverton fastened the top two buttons on his overcoat. "Thank you for your help, Daguerre. Please excuse me."

Mr. Beaverton shuffled up the stairs and through the main shop. "Leaving so soon, Mr. Beaverton?" Albert inquired as he set his remaining letters into the press.

"Yes, for now." Mr. Beaverton stopped at the door. "Oh, Albert?"

Albert glanced up. "Yes?"

"I would hold off publishing the identity of the thief. I don't think we have the whole story yet."

Albert returned to quickly setting the type. "Sure, Mr. Beaverton."

Mr. Beaverton sniffed the afternoon air as he left the shop. He took a few steps and felt something hard under his feet. He peered down. *Castor canadensis!* His new green buttons were strewn on the ground.

He slowly bent down to pick up each green button, a couple of which had just broken into several pieces. He put the pieces into his pocket and watched them fall to the ground again. *Paw slivers. . .* He pulled out the inside of his pocket to find an acorn-sized hole. He began to feel guilty as he squinted at the Howling Forest that loomed just beyond the creek. A layer of mist was lingering in the trees. *Sly couldn't have gone far. . .*

He scurried to the banks of Cobble Creek, dove into the water, and swam to the opposite side. He shook the water off his waistcoat and wandered towards the cloudy mist.

He breathed in the dampness of the trees, noting the unique smell of each species. His feet brushed over the dead pine needles covering the ground, with ferns and yellow, purple, and blue wildflowers sprinkling the edges of the path. He gripped his cane and used his sense of smell to see as he shuffled deeper into the darkening forest.

Mr. Beaverton cupped his paws around his mouth to amplify his voice. "Sly?" he called. He listened to birds chirping in the trees. "Sly? Can you hear me?"

He jumped as a pinecone landed on his head. He looked up towards the trees where two squirrels gave each other high fives and skittered away. "Hey there!" His voice echoed in the otherwise silent forest.

Mr. Beaverton waddled along the deserted forest path. Shadows bounced off the trees as squirrels leapt between the branches. He continued along the path, which began to disappear.

Suddenly, a large rustling of leaves and a squawk made him jump.

A red-tailed hawk swooped down from the trees onto a passerby. *Rubbery shrubs!* It was Sly.

"AHHH!" Sly yelled. "N–Nova?" Sly tried to dodge the hawk's claws.

Mr. Beaverton took a deep breath and gripped his cane. He inched closer to the hawk as it continued its attack on Sly. Right as Mr. Beaverton raised the cane, the hawk rotated her head. Mr. Beaverton jumped back and tripped over a root, causing him to lose his balance. As Mr. Beaverton fell, his cane launched from his flailing arms, hitting the hawk squarely on the head.

"Svwrckk!" The hawk, stunned from the blow, leapt off Sly. She glared at Mr. Beaverton for a moment and then turned her body to face Sly. "Watch your back, Sly! *Vipera is furious!*" The hawk spat before flying deeper into the forest.

Mr. Beaverton clutched his chest. "Are you all

right, Sly?"

Sly massaged his head. "Yes, I think so."

"Did you know that hawk? Nova, was it?"

Sly shivered. "I used to work with her, sort of." He stood and brushed his jacket. "What are you doing here, Beaverton?"

Mr. Beaverton held up the buttons. "I'm really sorry that I accused you, Sly."

Sly shrugged. "Well, I guess I haven't had the best business dealings since moving to Knotty Pine."

"Maybe you just need a better job," Mr. Beaverton suggested.

Sly studied Mr. Beaverton's expression and yipped a laugh. "Yes, I suppose. Maybe I'd work for you, if you ever had an interesting case."

Mr. Beaverton furrowed his brow. "Sly, I don't wish trouble for this town just to have an exciting career."

"Sometimes trouble comes on its own."

Mr. Beaverton bit his lip, thinking about the stolen objects and break-ins today. "I suppose."

Sly stood and brushed his jacket. "Well, thanks for saving me. I guess that cane came in handy after all."

Mr. Beaverton laughed. "Shall we go pay a visit to Toma? Before the hawk comes back, anyway."

Sly cautiously peered over his shoulder. "Sure."

11

The Thief

THE library sat on the other side of Hoover's Haberdashy and Mercantile and just before the schoolhouse. Mr. Beaverton and Sly crept into the small brick building. Sunlight peeked through the windows onto the tables and windowsills. Dust surrounded the books on the shelves that had been carved from tree branches and pine wood.

Toma peeked up from a stack of books at her desk. As they drew nearer, her eyes widened. She fled for the hole leading to her underground den.

"Toma!" Mr. Beaverton called as she disappeared into the hole just the right size for a woodrat. He heard a rustling and then silence. He noticed a familiar odor in the air.

Sly and Mr. Beaverton peered into the hole. The room was packed full of thimbles, bells, cups, feathers, and colorful fabrics. Mr. Beaverton noticed the tip of a fork and the handle of a pail.

"Tooooma! We need to speak with you!" Mr. Beaverton's voice echoed.

Sly leaned closer to the hole. "We see the stolen silver and the," he rolled his eyes, *"lunch pail."*

Toma poked her head through the entrance of her room, her eyes wide with fear.

"I... I was coerced into stealing!" she squeaked.

"What?" Mr. Beaverton scrunched his brow.

Toma drummed her foot nervously. "Miss Di... she persuaded me to steal."

Mr. Beaverton shook his head in disbelief. "That's absurd." Miss Di had always been a loyal, trustworthy secretary. Although, she had been acting a little off today.

Mr. Beaverton looked back at Toma as she waved her paws in the air. "She said there's a... a dangerous snake coming! A—a viper!"

"Oh no..." Sly whispered.

Mr. Beaverton turned to Sly questioningly and then to the door of the library as it swung open. Oscar and Quilliver marched in.

"Mr. Beaverton! We've been searchin' everywhere for you!" Oscar shouted.

"Oscar? What's going on?" Mr. Beaverton asked.

Suddenly, Miss Di barreled through the doorway and into the room. "Wait, Mr. Beaverton! I can explain!"

"Quilliver was cleanin' the library chimney for his after school job," Oscar interrupted, "and found this letter in the ashes from Miss Di," Oscar pointed at

Miss Di, "to Toma. Miss Di *asked* Toma to steal ev'ryone's stuff today!"

Quilliver stepped forward. "Here—here is the letter, Mr. Beaverton." He handed him a small piece of parchment covered in black soot.

Mr. Beaverton took the letter and turned to Miss Di. "Is this true?"

"Yes, Mr. Beaverton. . ." She sighed. "But it's—it's not fair."

"What's not fair?" Mr. Beaverton asked.

She put her paw on her hip. "I've been your secretary for *two years*, and you've never asked me to help with more than taking notes and *filing reports.*"

Mr. Beaverton nodded, remembering the mystery novel on her desk this morning. "I had no idea you were interested in detective work. You never told me."

Miss Di's eyes grew round. "Mr. Beaverton, you've never noticed before? My dream has always been to work in forensics. Oh, Mr. Beaverton, I could inspect suspicious items you find. And I can climb trees to survey for evidence."

Mr. Beaverton massaged his forehead. "Yes, I suppose that would be helpful. But, Miss Di, I need to know why you asked Toma to steal around town."

"Oh Toma, you know how she can't resist anything shiny." Miss Di motioned to Toma, who was
bobbing her head up and down. "And anything green.
I paid her with pistachios. Anyway, I needed a reason to investigate around town. Knotty Pine hasn't
had any good mysteries since those acorn robbers and
your grandfather's disappearance. I thought if I could
prove to you. . ."

"Wait," Mr. Beaverton put a paw up. "We found
Toma's fur in the schoolyard, Topsy Turvy's Restaurant, and the print shop. Why those places?"

"I figured the schoolyard and print shop were clos-
est to the outskirts of town, and visitors often come
to the restaurant," Miss Di replied.

"Visitors? So, if Toma stole the pail, silver, and
letters, who stole from you?" Mr. Beaverton asked.

"Well. . ." Miss Di said as she sheepishly brought
the gold-tipped quill from her pouch.

Mr. Beaverton furrowed his brow, staring at the
gold-tipped quill. "But, who broke the pitcher. . . and
stunned you?"

She coughed nervously. "I did. I mean, I broke the
pitcher and then waited in the office on the ground.
I needed you to believe that we were really having a

town crisis."

Mr. Beaverton rubbed his aching head. "You told a real thumper, Miss Di."

"What?"

He put his face in his paw. "You really tricked us." He looked up. "Who broke into Hoover's?"

Miss Di tilted her head. "Hoover's? What are you talking about?"

"You didn't have Toma break into Hoover's?"

"No, I didn't," Miss Di insisted.

Mr. Beaverton blew out a breath. "Odd."

Miss Di twisted her paws. "But, I'm not telling you everything."

Mr. Beaverton sighed, trying to remain calm. *"Please* explain, Miss Di! Why were you checking the outskirts of town? Why the concern over visitors?"

She dropped her shoulders. "I... you received a telegraph early this morning."

"Go on..." Mr. Beaverton's heart sunk into his stomach.

Miss Di pulled a small note out of her pouch. "Morse received a telegraph from Sheriff Ovis for you and passed it on to me, as he usually does. The escaped inmate, Vipera Berus, was spotted in Derwood.

Sheriff thinks she is heading our way."

Mr. Beaverton spun around as he heard a gasp behind him. "Sly, are you okay?

Sly sat on the ground. "I... I have to leave."

"What are you talking about?" Mr. Beaverton sputtered. "Ever since a snake was mentioned..."

"I should have realized with the snakeskin... and the hawk. But I couldn't believe that she could actually be *here.*" Sly stared at his paws.

"Sly, you're not making sense. Please explain," Mr. Beaverton said firmly.

Sly wiped his forehead. "I worked for Vipera when I moved to England a couple years ago. My cousin got me a job mixing nuts, which is how the pistachio-betel fiasco began. You know betel nuts are green like pistachios but poisonous."

Mr. Beaverton stepped forward. "What brought you to Knotty Pine, Sly?"

"When Vipera and some of her employees were on trial, I wasn't caught, because I was always working in the back of the warehouse. So, she sent me to find the animal who turned her in to the police." He gulped. "A hedgehog who bought the nuts for his mercantile."

Mr. Beaverton raised his eyebrows. "A hedge-hog?"

"She promised me a reward, but I never returned to her. And... I may have taken a few crates of pistachios... which is why I need to leave if she's here." Sly stood. "Vipera isn't just deceptive and greedy. I know her... she gets even."

"Sly, did you find the hedgehog?" Mr. Beaverton pressed.

Sly looked at his feet. "Yes, I followed him here a few months ago. And he's still here."

Mr. Beaverton blew out a sharp breath. "Hoover."

12

The Rescue

"SLY, you can't just leave!" Mr. Beaverton exclaimed. "Hoover might be in trouble."

"Beaverton, you don't understand. This snake—she's ruthless. She burned down her own warehouse just to cover up that she had betel nuts, and she didn't even *warn* us beforehand." He shivered.

Miss Di stepped forward. "I'm not afraid. I'll go."

Mr. Beaverton shook his head. "You've caused enough chaos today. I don't need you hurt. And," he frowned, "if I hadn't been so distracted today following Toma, I might have been more aware that Hoover was in danger."

"But Mr. Beaverton, I checked all the corners and baskets around town, all places that snakes like to hide. I was going to find the snake..." Miss Di explained.

Mr. Beaverton wiped at the sweat forming on his brow. "There's no time for discussion. I'm going to go check on Hoover." He turned to Oscar. "You and Quilliver should accompany Miss Di back to her den and make sure it's safe." Mr. Beaverton scurried out the door.

"Be careful, Mr. Beaverton!" Oscar yelled after him.

Mr. Beaverton paused in front of Hoover's doorway and drank a little of the mint extract that Lady Eden had given him earlier that day. He felt awake and alert, and *he might need to be.*

He pushed the door to the mercantile open. The fur on his neck stood up as the bell on the door rang. The shop was still and silent. His eyes skimmed the fabrics and thread to the buttons and baskets, all neatly arranged on the shelves.

He slowly peered behind the counter. Spilled baskets and shattered porcelain lined the ground.

He shuffled to the back. Just as he walked around

the corner, a tip of a tail cuffed him in the face. As he fell to the ground he tried to focus his eyes, but a second blow made his vision slowly go dark.

*   *   *

Young Beaverton stared at the flowing water of Cobble Creek. He leapt into the water, dropping several sticks that he had gathered. He quickly attempted to retrieve as many as he could before they floated away. He climbed out of the water, empty pawed, and shook his fur under the sun. He stared down the river at Grandfather's pristine lodge, strong and unyielding to the current.

"Haven't gotten started yet?" Grandfather spoke behind him.

"My lodge will never be as strong as yours."

Grandfather laughed. "Nonsense! Choose the sturdiest logs and swim powerfully against that river current every day, and you'll have a Beaverton-worthy lodge in no time."

"If I could just get enough sticks out there..."

Grandfather leaned on his cane. "Come now, persistence makes you strong. And we're here if you need us." He picked up a stick and handed it to him.

"*We?*"

Grandfather smiled. "*Always me, and also the good citizens of Knotty Pine. Remember that.*"

Remember that. Remember that.

* * *

Mr. Beaverton groggily awoke with a slight hissing in his ear. "Grandfather?" He slapped at his head. As his vision cleared, he began to make out gold and black scaly skin wrapped around his feet. He felt a sharp intake of breath as his eyes bulged.

"Hellooo, Mr. Beaverton." Mr. Beaverton stared into the yellow eyes of a European viper, venomous and fierce. He tried to wiggle his feet, but they were tightly bound by the body of the snake. A few paces away, an animal hovered in the corner: Hoover.

"W-what do you want?" Mr. Beaverton tried to keep his voice steady.

"Wellll, I only wanted the hedgehog," the snake whispered, "untilll you willingly joined usss."

Hoover curled into a ball. "M'm –orry, Mr. – eaverton."

"You must be that wicked snake we've been hearing about!" Mr. Beaverton swallowed and tried to inch from Vipera's grasp as she tightened her tail.

"Indeed, I am. Vipera Berusss, from the British Islesss."

Mr. Beaverton gazed at her vertical pupils and sleek skin. Vipera was as radiant as she was danger-ous. He cleared his throat. "You traveled all the way here, from Europe? *Why?*"

Vipera struck at the air just an inch from Hoover's quivering body. "I *TOLD* youuu—the *hedgehog.*"

The back door burst open. Sly, Miss Di, and Oscar ran into the room. "COME ANY CLOSER, and I'll ssssink my fangsss into Hoover," Vipera hissed.

"Let him go, Vipera!" Sly shouted.

Vipera's nose flared as she focused on Sly. "Staaay out of this, Ssssepluv. I haven't even gotten started with you and your disssloyalty." Sly retreated into a corner with Oscar and Miss Di.

Oscar threw a fish at Vipera's head. She narrowed her eyes in response. "Real maturrrrre."

Mr. Beaverton looked from his feet to his clammy paws, considering using his claws to scratch at the snake. "So you came all this way, just for Hoover?"

Vipera flicked her tongue. "Care to explain *why*, Hoover?"

Hoover trembled as he slightly uncurled and shifted his eyes to Mr. Beaverton. "Early last year, I lived in England and had a mercantile there, much like I have here. I was a fairly new business owner and didn't have much experience finding good suppliers. I received a couple of recommendations to try Vipera. She traded me the 'up and coming' pistachio for a great deal. I–I didn't realize I was really making my customers sick with the betel nut."

Vipera hissed into Hoover's face. "Continuuuuue."

"After more than one customer ended up in the hospital, I took the matter to the police and exposed her entire operation in the process. She was likely going to prison," Hoover finished.

Hoover turned to the snake. "But please, Vipera!"

She snapped her fangs. "No one getsss away with crossssing me!" She brought her head closer to Hoover.

Mr. Beaverton stopped wiggling his feet. "But why, Vipera?"

She whipped her head up and focused on Mr. Beaverton. "Why what?" Droplets of rain began to pound on the roof as she glowered at him.

Mr. Beaverton shifted nervously. "Why sell the

betel nut with the pistachio? Hoover here said they're much bigger. You weren't going to get away with it for long."

"Most animalsss are denssse," She murmured. "They don't pay attention while they *devour* their food."

Mr. Beaverton straightened. "Animals are *not* dense, and they are becoming aware now."

Vipera's mouth curled up. "I've already infiltrated the trading systemsss. I'll get the betel nut out, even if it's in slightly smaller quantitiesss, and continue to make my fortune."

"So, it's all about wealth." Mr. Beaverton's nostrils flared, thinking of all those sick animals.

Vipera's gaze grew darker as she lifted her head. "I had nothing as a hatchling. Sure, pick on the viper because she's small, because she's poor. Well now I have wealth," she exposed her fangs, "and *power.*"

Just as Vipera opened her mouth to strike Hoover, Mr. Beaverton slammed his cane down onto her tail.

The ferocious snake screeched as her tail writhed. "AHHHHHHHHHGGAAAAAAAGGGG!"

Vipera's grip loosened, and Mr. Beaverton took the opportunity to free himself. Vipera tried to strike

CHAPTER TWELVE

him as he moved to save Hoover. Mr. Beaverton dodged her and stumbled into the corner towards Sly, Oscar, and Miss Di.

Suddenly, Miss Di climbed onto a barrel and leapt to a nearby shelf. Then she sprang right onto the back of the snake with her claws exposed. Vipera shrieked and snapped her fangs at Miss Di. Miss Di dug her claws in deeper. Vipera quivered in pain.

Vipera finally contorted her head close enough to bite Miss Di, but the snake was paralyzed by Miss Di's grip.

Vipera turned from Hoover as she put her energy into biting Miss Di's shoulder. Miss Di yelped from the bite and fell from overexertion.

As Vipera examined her wound, Hoover scampered around her to the door. Vipera hissed as Hoover darted out of his shop. "You can't esssscape *ME!*" She slithered desperately towards the door, her injuries slowing her down.

Hoover paused briefly in the center of town as rain poured around him. He jumped at a clap of thunder and disappeared towards the Howling Forest.

"Hoooover!" Vipera screamed as she slithered into the darkened town. The wind whipped angrily around her.

"Vipera!" She pivoted her head back to the shop right as Mr. Beaverton launched a heavy barrel of corn kernels towards her. She jerked as the heavy barrel hit her head. The kernels sprang into the air and bounced all over the ground.

Vipera lay still under the barrel.

Mr. Beaverton heaved a breath. He then gasped at the sight of Miss Di who was still lying on the ground of the mercantile.

"Miss Di!" Mr. Beaverton sprinted to her side.

"Someone get Dr. Hoot!"

Miss Di coughed. "No, the snake," she said as she tried to sit up.

"Miss Di, please, lie down," Mr. Beaverton directed.

"No! I'm fine." She coughed again. "Get Vipera locked up—now!"

Mr. Beaverton pursed his lips. "You're not fine! You were bit. Look how red it is."

Miss Di laughed. "Don't you know, Mr. Beaverton? Opossums are immune to snake venom."

"What! Immune?" Mr. Beaverton asked quickly.

"Now get that snake locked up! I'm too tired to attack her again."

"Wow, Miss Di. . ." Mr. Beaverton said in awe.

Sly and Oscar carefully dragged the viper to the town prison. They put her into a cage with acorn-sized holes so she could not slither out.

Dr. Hoot came to assist Mr. Beaverton and Miss Di.

Dr. Hoot examined Miss Di's wound. "You know, the best way to treat a lesion like this is to clean it thoroughly and. . ."

Suddenly, Lady Eden burst into the room with a

basket full of herbs. "I came as quickly as I could." She pulled out an herb, facing Miss Di. "These juniper leaves can help with any injury."

"Uh, thank you, Lady Eden..." Dr. Hoot shrugged and rummaged through his bag.

"Dr. Hoot?" Mr. Beaverton tried to stand, but he stumbled over his feet.

"Please, Beaverton, lie down," Dr. Hoot ordered.

Mr. Beaverton sighed. "It's my foot, Doc. I must have reinjured it."

Dr. Hoot brought his spectacles down as he examined Mr. Beaverton's foot.

"I warned you, those paw slivers can get infected..."

"No, not that—I never had any—oh, never mind!" He took a breath. "Anyway, I injured my foot several months ago..." He faced Dr. Hoot. "You don't remember, Doc?"

"Sorry, I don't." Dr. Hoot brought some bandages out of his bag.

"But that accident—my grandfather..."

Dr. Hoot snapped his head up. "Your grandfather? Have you heard from him?"

"No, Doc. I don't even know if he's alive," Mr. Beaverton said softly, "Why would he leave?"

Dr. Hoot sighed. "I don't know. Get some rest, Beaverton."

He would solve the mystery of his grandfather's disappearance. *He had to.* Mr. Beaverton closed his eyes in exhaustion.

13

Pistachios

— One day later —

"WELL Mr. Beaverton, I think you succeeded in keeping the town safe. I didn't know we'd have a big-time criminal in our little town of Knotty Pine, or I wouldn't have left in the first place." Sheriff Ovis said as he sat in his office at the entrance of the jail.

"Thank you, Sheriff. Once we realized who Vipera was after, we were able to find and capture her. Thanks to Miss Di."

"Yes, Miss Di—she seems to be quite the secretary."

Mr. Beaverton nodded. "Hopefully more than

that now. If Miss Di hadn't distracted Vipera, Hoover might not be alive. She demonstrated that she was effective at more than taking notes. She's a bricky opossum."

"What?"

"Oh, bricky—another word for courageous," Mr. Beaverton explained.

"Well, wonderful!" Sheriff Ovis exclaimed.

Mr. Beaverton shifted in his chair. "So, Derwood all in order now?"

"Yes, the break-ins were from Vipera. She was certainly right under our snouts. She was spotted a few hours after I arrived that night. I sent the telegraph right away."

Mr. Beaverton scrunched his brow. "But, why was she breaking in?"

"Hunting for our mercantile owner, I presume," Sheriff Ovis said.

"And now that she's behind bars. . ."

"We'll arrange to transfer her back to England," Sheriff Ovis finished.

Mr. Beaverton tapped the desk. "How about the pistachios? Is the world safe from the betel nut?"

Sheriff Ovis moved some papers. "Our valley, at least. Vipera expanded so much that it's hard to tell which companies are safe to trade with. But, certainly any company attached to the name 'Berus' is one to avoid." He paused and brought out a bag. "But just in case. . ."

Sheriff Ovis pulled out a small red bag and poured out a pile of green nuts: some smaller and some larger. He popped one of the smaller nuts into his mouth. "Mmm. . ."

Mr. Beaverton gasped. "Are those—"

"Sir Sly Sepluv was just by. He was kind enough to provide me a sample of both the betel nut and the pistachio. I even convinced him to teach the citizens of Knotty Pine the difference, though it will cost me a few yards of silk. . ."

Mr. Beaverton chuckled. "I guess Sly is just full of surprises."

"Yes. I had received a tip from neighboring towns that he was a bit of a swindler, but I had no idea he was involved with Vipera," Sheriff Ovis added.

"It turns out she wasn't very pleased with him," Mr. Beaverton commented.

Sheriff Ovis nodded as he popped another pistachio into his mouth. "So, Hoover has disappeared?"

"Yes, we haven't seen him since yesterday. He escaped from Vipera into the Howling Forest," Mr. Beaverton explained.

Sheriff Ovis glanced out the window. "Well, I'll send Corvus to find him."

Mr. Beaverton stood. "I think I'll be going, Sheriff."

"Thanks again, Mr. Beaverton. I know I can rely on you to keep Knotty Pine safe."

Mr. Beaverton walked out into the sunshine over the center of town. The ground was damp under his feet from last night's storm. He grinned at Sly, who was standing with his arms folded in front of the Pine Lodge.

"I hope you're satisfied with yourself," Sly smirked.

"Quite so. First 'real' case in Knotty Pine solved with the sheriff's approval."

Sly nodded. "Glad you can agree that a missing lunch pail isn't a catastrophe."

"Well, perhaps it is here." Mr. Beaverton cocked his head. "So, what made you stay yesterday? You were going to leave."

Sly shrugged. "I felt like I'd need to face Berus eventually, and I might as well get it over with."

"Thank you, Sly. I really couldn't have done it without your... sarcasm," Mr. Beaverton said. Sly snorted.

"I'm kidding! But really, you, Miss Di, and Oscar—you all helped in your own way..." Mr. Beaverton began.

"Beaverton, really."

"Fine. Oh, and here." Mr. Beaverton pulled a parcel out of his pocket. "The silk."

Sly gave a toothy grin. "I guess I earned it. What

now, Beaverton?"

"To begin, I think you should continue to assist me on any mysteries here in this town, especially if the crimes become more serious. I worry for the future of Knotty Pine. And two..." Mr. Beaverton paused and sniffed the air.

"Mr. Beaverton!" Lady Eden ran to them, her eyes wide.

"What is it?"

"Black smoke, rising from the Bluebird Mountains!"

Mr. Beaverton gasped, whipping his head to the forest. *"Splinters from an aspen tree!* Are you sure?"

"It's still far, but coming closer," Lady Eden's voice quivered.

"Lady Eden! Please sound the warning bell at the school at once!"

Mr. Beaverton turned to Sly. "It looks like Knotty Pine still needs us. What do you say, Sly? Are you coming?"

Sly made a face. "No lunch pails?"

"No lunch pails." Mr. Beaverton pointed his cane towards the mountains. "Off we go!"

Epilogue

VIPERA hissed in her cell. *They will pay. They will ALL pay.*

Suddenly, a crash made her jolt. She squinted her eyes in the darkness at pointy ears and a long snout.

"Whoo iss it?"

The stranger smirked and stepped closer to the light in her cell. "I've come to free you."

Evergreen Valley

CRYSTA

HICKORY

MUIR
MEADOW

DERWOOD

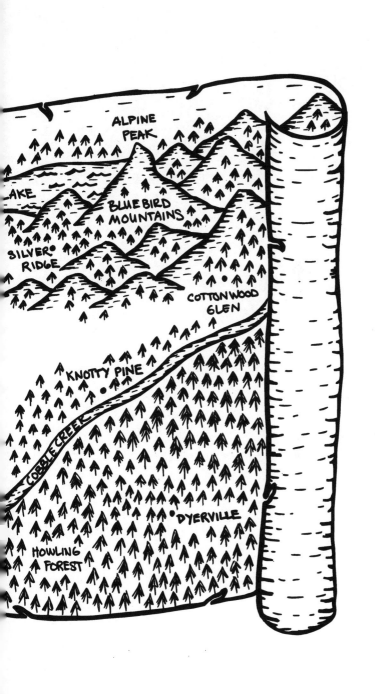

Glossary

alpine forget-me-nots: a bluish-purple flower found in the mountains (and Miss Di's favorite).

arson: the act of purposely setting fire to someone's property.

aspen: a type of tree common to North America that has smooth, whitish-gray bark. Mr. Beaverton loves to eat bark from this type of tree.

beaver: a large rodent known for building lodges and dams in rivers and keeping land fertile. They like to eat the inner bark of trees.

betel nut: the seed from a certain type of palm tree. The nut produces a burst of energy but also has negative health side effects.

big-horned sheep: a species of sheep known for their large horns.

bolt: a board around which fabric is wrapped for storage.

breeches: an 1800's word for pants.

British Isles: islands located off the coast of Europe and the birthplace of Hoover and Vipera.

buckram: a coarse cloth often used to cover and protect books.

caper: a far-fetched story.

***Castor canadensis*:** the scientific name for the North American beaver and one of Mr. Beaverton's common exclamations.

catastrophe: a disaster. In Knotty Pine, this may be something as simple as a missing lunch pail (do you hear that? A faint groan from Sir Sly...).

chicory: a type of flower from the dandelion family. Chicory are found near the Knotty Pine schoolhouse.

chipmunk: a small, striped rodent.

colubrid: a classification of snakes that are generally considered harmless. Most colubrids either do not carry venom or carry venom that is harmless to humans.

commonplace book: the name for a type of notebook used in the 1800s to compile letters, poems, quotes, etc. Miss Di uses hers to record her notes for her police reports (and her investigative observations).

cornflower: a bluish-purple flower.

cottonwood: a fast-growing tree that can be used to make newspaper.

cravat: a decorative cloth worn around the neck and a predecessor to the modern necktie.

crow: a black-colored bird belonging to the *Corvus* genus.

daguerreotype: a photograph produced by the process of Daguerreotypy. The process was invented in the 1800s and used silver-plated copper plates and iodine to generate grayscale images.

den: a shelter or home for an animal that is often underground or in a hollowed-out area. Miss Di's den is below Mr. Beaverton's office.

eastern box turtle: a turtle with an orange, hinged shell that is native to the Eastern United States.

eating chamber: a section in a beaver lodge used for eating.

escargot ('ess-car-go'):   a cooked snail, usually served at the beginning of a meal.

faux ('foe'):   a fake or imitation of something genuine.

forensics: techniques for analyzing a crime scene to determine how and by whom the crime was committed. Miss Di studies forensics in her spare time.

great-horned owl: a large owl with a loud call.

haberdashery: a store where objects used for sewing such as buttons and ribbons are sold.

hedgehog: a spiny mammal found in Europe.

heirloom: an object of value that is passed down through time from one family member to another.

herb: a plant used for food or medicine such as mint or juniper.

huckleberry: a purplish berry and the primary ingredient in the Topsy Turvy Special.

immune: to be resistant to the dangerous effects of a normally harmful substance. Interestingly, opossums are immune to the venom of many snakes.

jackrabbit: a mammal similar to the rabbit but with taller hind legs and longer ears.

knoll: a grassy hill.

lodge: a beaver's home made with sticks and grass. The structure usually includes a feeding chamber, a nesting chamber, and two underwater entrances.

mercantile: a store where general goods like food and clothing are sold or traded.

mint: a plant used in traditional medicine to calm upset stomachs and relieve pain. Mr. Beaverton believes mint enhances his concentration.

mountain cottontail rabbit: a type of rabbit found in the mountains of North America.

mountain laurel: an evergreen shrub with light pink and white flowers.

mussel: an animal found near water that lives in an oval-shaped shell. The animals in Knotty Pine use empty mussel shells as buttons for their clothing.

mustachioed: to have a long mustache.

nocturnal: animals that sleep during the day and are active at night, such as Ms. Olug the wolverine.

opossum: a small gray and white marsupial and the only marsupial native to North America. Like koala bears and kangaroos, female opossums have a pouch on their stomachs that they use to carry their young and keep them safe. Miss Di uses her pouch to carry her commonplace book and quill.

pantaloons: pants that are baggy from the waist to the lower leg but tight near the ankles.

pawn: someone who others use to their advantage. Sly insults Mr. Beaverton by calling him the Sheriff's pawn.

penny-farthing bicycle: a type of bicycle with a large front wheel and a small rear wheel that was commonly used in the 1800s. Oscar rides his penny-farthing around Knotty Pine.

pinstripe: a pattern of thin, parallel stripes on clothing.

pistachio: a green nut with a soft shell. Imported pistachios became popular in the United States in the late 1800s.

porcupine: a small mammal that carries barbed quills on their body.

predicament: a difficult situation, such as the break-ins that occur in Derwood or when Sheriff Ovis' boat nearly dismantles Mr. Beaverton's lodge.

printing press: a device used in the 1800s to apply ink to paper or cloth.

quill: 1. a feather whose tip may be dipped in ink and used for writing. Miss Di's quill has a golden tip. 2. the sharp spines on a porcupine.

red fox: a dog-like mammal that enjoys digging.

red-tailed hawk: a bird with a brownish-red tail that eats small animals like rodents.

river otter: a mammal common in North America that lives partly in water and partly on land. River otters are playful and love to eat.

setting type: the process of loading small metal letters into a printing press in preparation for producing a print.

silk: a stringy material produced by silkworms that may be woven into cloth.

silo: a tall cylinder used to store food. The animals of Knotty Pine store acorns and other nuts in the town silo.

smock: an apron.

snail: a small, sticky creature that has no bones but wears a hard shell.

snakeskin: a papery outer layer of a snake's skin that is shed a few times per year.

spectacles: another term for eyeglasses

spines: prickly strands of fur on a hedgehog. The spines of a hedgehog are approximately the same length over the entire surface of their body.

swindle: to use trickery and dishonesty to sell goods.

telegraph: a system used in the 1800s for sending messages over an electrical wire, usually by a pattern of long and short signals called morse code. Morse the skunk runs the telegraph in Knotty Pine.

thanatosis: also known as "apparent death," thanatosis is a coma-like defensive state used by some animals such as opossums when they shocked or stunned. Opossums produce an excess of drool in this state.

thimble: a metal cap used to protect the fingers or thumbs when sewing.

tracks: an imprint made in the dirt or snow by an animal.

twill sack: a sack made with a woven fabric.

verbena: a type of flower that comes in a variety of colors including blue, pink, red, and white.

vial: a small glass container often used to store a drug or chemical.

***Vipera berus*:** the scientific name for the common European viper.

vulpicide: the act of killing a fox.

waistcoat: a sleeveless coat with buttons.

wolverine: a small, bear-like animal that is known to be aggressive.

woodrat: a rat-like rodent that has a bushy tail. Woodrats love to gather and store items and are also known as "packrats."

yard: an English unit of length equal to three feet.

yellow-bellied marmot: a large ground squirrel with a yellow belly.

Reflection Questions

1. Have you ever lost something important to you? Did you find it?

2. If Sly had sold a rotten or broken product to you, but later asked for forgiveness, would you give him a second chance?

3. Oscar went out of his way to warn Mr. Beaverton about the snakeskin and Mr. Beaverton was too busy to go look at it. How would you feel if you were Oscar?

4. Mr. Beaverton's grandfather used to say, "Our town is like a lodge—each town member is a stick or branch that keeps us all together." What do you think Grandfather Beaverton was trying to say?

5. How was Mr. Beaverton brave in "The Rescue"? How was Sly brave? Miss Di?

About the Author   Olivia Rian wrote her first book when she was seven, a comic book called "The Pimple-Faced Dragon" (poor dragon).   After surviving a few frosty winters in the Mountain West, she received a degree in English from Brigham Young University–Idaho. She now lives in the DC metropolitan area, closer to her original home in the Midwest.   Olivia enjoys reading, shopping, biking, baking dessert, and making trips to the beach with her husband and two kids.

About the Illustrator   Sara Aycock is a stay-at-home mother of three by day and an artist by night (those close to her know she is a night owl). She enjoys spending time outdoors, especially in the forest, with her husband and children. Sara has always felt a strong connection to nature, and it is often the subject of her artwork. Sara uses her artwork to express her thoughts and feelings: "As I create art, it becomes part of who I am; as I share my art, it becomes part of who you are."

See more of Sara's art at: SaraAycockArt.etsy.com

Made in the USA
San Bernardino, CA
30 July 2017